ScHooL FoR Little MoNsters

First published in 2017 by Scholastic Children's Books

Euston House, 24 Eversholt Street, London NW1 1DB

a division of Scholastic Ltd

www.scholastic.co.uk

London ~ New York ~ Toronto ~ Sydney ~ Auckland ~ Mexico City ~ New Delhi ~ Hong Kong

Text copyright © 2017 Michelle Robinson   Illustrations copyright © 2017 Sarah Horne

ISBN 978 1 4071 6534 9

Printed in Malaysia

10 9 8 7 6 5 4 3 2 1

The moral rights of Michelle Robinson and Sarah Horne have been asserted.

Papers used by Scholastic Children's Books are made from wood grown in sustainable forests.

TO ALL AT TRINITY FIRST SCHOOL, FROME

M.R.

FOR IRIS

S.H.

Michelle Robinson

Sarah Horne

SCHOOL FOR Little MoNSters

SCHOLASTIC

Side by side there stand two schools.
Each with **VERY** different rules.
Bob and Blob both start today.
Let's hope they get inside okay…

Uh-oh... **monsters**!
Everywhere!
They've swapped the signs round.
That's not fair!

NICE SCHOOL.
FOR BOYS AND GIRLS

Will Bob and Blob

both know the way?

Of course not - this is their first day!

Well, *you* might pick the wrong front door
if you'd not been to school before.

It's hard when everything is new.
The **RULES** will tell them what to do.

When your name's called,
say, "I'm here."

OUR WORK

Write as neatly
as you're able.

PENS

my name is
James. I like
football

I li... mum
say...

RULE 2

Dawdle.
Doodle
on the table.

RULE 2

Draw a picture of your mum.

RULE 3

Add a really MASSIVE bum.

RULE 3

Break time, kids.

Let's have a snack.

Number practice –

eight, nine, ten…

RULE 6

How many BOGIES on your pen?

RULE 6

Don't be shy at Show and Tell.

RULE 7 Share a really NASTY smell.

Take a plate and wait in line.

RULE 8

Grab the best bits.
Holler, "MINE!"

RULE 8

Eat your lunch.

Sit nice and still.

RULE 9

Giggle. Wriggle. Belch at will.

No calling names.

No picking fights.

RULE 10

Work really hard
and *try your best.*

RULE 11

RULE 11

WEE BOTTOMS BOGIES

Write "BOTTOMS" on your spelling test.

At Story Time
be *quiet*, please.

RULE 12

TRUMP, then say, "Who cut the cheese?"

RULE 12

Just *ask* if you need the loo.

GOLD STAR
for the biggest poo.

RULE 13

Greet your grown-up at the door.

RULE 14

When you spot them, give a ROAR.

RULE 14

Wasn't Day One lots of fun?

Your adventure's just begun.

You'll learn and grow at school each day.

Just choose the RIGHT one, kids. Okay?